This one's for you, Kathy Ricke. OOGA!—T. S.

For my mom and dad, who never said no to a pet.—B. S.

SIMON & SCHUSTER BOOKS FOR YOUNG READERS
An imprint of Simon & Schuster Children's Publishing Division
1230 Avenue of the Americas, New York, New York 10020
Text copyright © 2012 by Tammi Sauer
Illustrations copyright © 2012 by Bob Shea
SIMON & SCHUSTER BOOKS FOR YOUNG READERS is a trademark of Simon & Schuster, Inc.
For information about special discounts for bulk purchases, please contact Simon & Schuster
Special Sales at 1-866-506-1949 or business@simonandschuster.com.
The Simon & Schuster Speakers Bureau can bring authors to your live event. For more information
or to book an event, contact the Simon & Schuster Speakers Bureau at 1-866-248-3049 or
visit our website at www.simonspeakers.com.
Book design by Lucy Ruth Cummins
The text for this book is set in Grit Primer.
The illustrations for this book are rendered digitally.
Manufactured in China
1211 SCP
10 9 8 7 6 5 4 3 2 1
Library of Congress Cataloging-in-Publication Data
Sauer, Tammi.
Me want pet! / Tammi Sauer ; illustrated by Bob Shea.—1st ed.
p. cm.
"A Paula Wiseman Book."
Summary: When Cave Boy wants a pet, he tries a woolly mammoth, a saber-toothed tiger, and a dodo bird,
but none seems suitable.
ISBN 978-1-4424-0810-4 (hardcover)
[1. Cave dwellers—Fiction. 2. Extinct animals—Fiction. 3. Pets—Fiction.] I. Shea, Bob, ill. II. Title.
PZ7.S2502Me 2012
[E]—dc22
2010019500

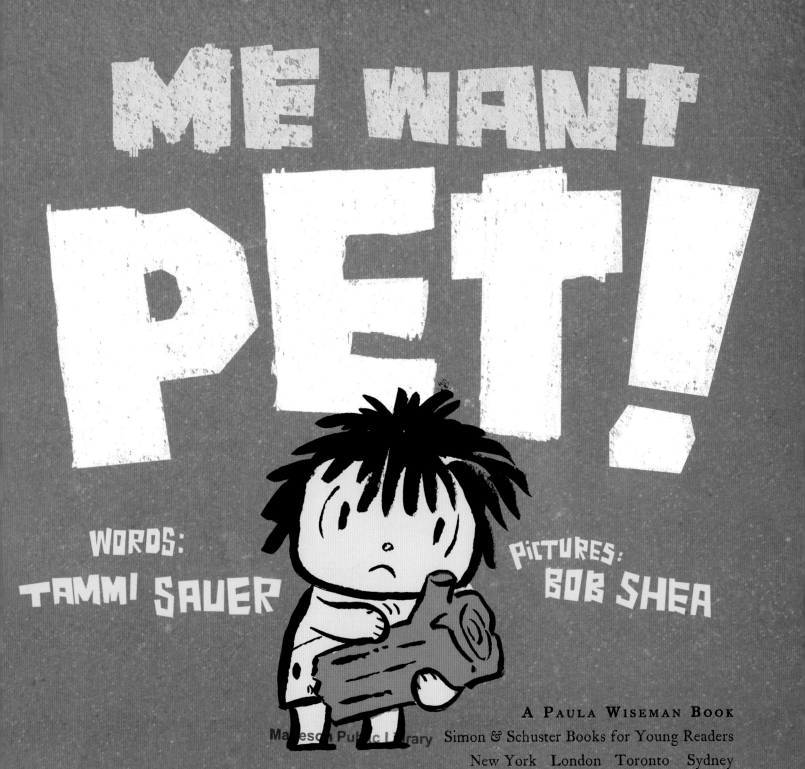

ME WANT PET!

WORDS:
TAMMI SAUER

PICTURES:
BOB SHEA

A PAULA WISEMAN BOOK
Simon & Schuster Books for Young Readers
New York   London   Toronto   Sydney

Cave Boy had lots of things.

Rocks.

Sticks.

A club.

But no pet.

"Me sad," said Cave Boy. "Want pet."

Cave Boy went to find one.

He searched near

and far

until . . .

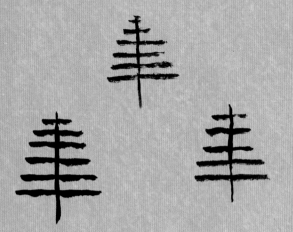

a woolly mammoth!

Cave Boy
rode
Woolly
home.

"Me want pet!"

"Ug,"
grunted Mama.
"He too big.
Where he sleep?"

Cave Boy gave Woolly a hug.
"Me wish you could stay, pal."

Then Cave Boy tried again.

He searched high

and low until . . .

a saber-toothed tiger!

Cave Boy and Toothy raced home.

Cave Boy and Toothy sighed.
"Me sorry, buddy."

But Cave Boy did not give up.

He searched across grasslands.

Over seas.

And through forests.

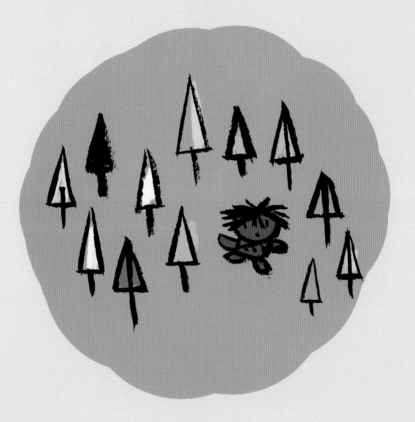

"Poor baby," said Cave Boy.
"No mama anywhere."

"WAH-WAH!"

"No too big. No sneeze.
ME WANT PET!"

"Ug," grunted Gran.
"No can keep! He no potty-trained."

Cave Boy groaned and turned to Dodo.

"Me so sad. . . ."

Just then the ground shook.

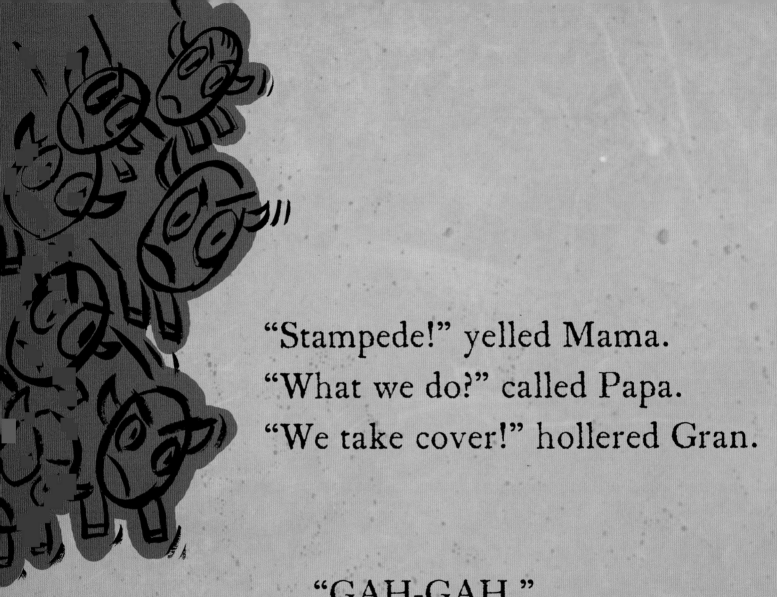

"Stampede!" yelled Mama.
"What we do?" called Papa.
"We take cover!" hollered Gran.

"GAH-GAH."

"Dodo!"

Cave Boy to the rescue!

(With a little help
from his friends.)

"Phew-ga!" cheered the family.

Cave Boy had lots of things.

Rocks.

Sticks.

A club.

But Cave Boy did not have one pet.

Cave Boy had three.

OOGA!